This book belongs to

....

the World's Greatest
Mum

Put a photo
of your own
Mum here.

→

Written by Kath Smith
Illustrated by Steve Lavis
Designed by Chris Fraser at Page to Page

This is a Parragon Book
First published in 2005

Parragon
Queen Street House
4 Queen Street
Bath BA1 1HE, UK

ISBN 1-40544-421-5

Printed in China

World's Greatest
Mum

Written by Kath Smith Illustrated by Steve Lavis

p

I'm so glad my mum belongs to me!

She gives the best ever cuddles in the world...

...and the best ever presents –
like this great camera!

Mum says I'll soon get the hang of it!

Here are some pictures of Bonnie, my dog. I don't think she likes my camera.

My mum is brilliant at making things...

...and mending things, too!

Mum made this dragon costume for my party.

But the tail was a bit long.

Mum's a fantastic cook, too. I think she makes the yummiest snacks...

Just look at what we had at my birthday party!

Bonnie thinks my mum is a good cook, too!

Can you guess how old I am?

...and cakes. But she does need my help to decorate them!

Sometimes I feel a bit shy when there are lots of people around...

This is Jack and Lucy from school.

This is my best friend Milly and her mum.

James lives next door to me.

...but Mum is always there to help me out.

My mum can do anything!

She made a sword for Jack.

At my party Mum made things for everyone out of balloons.

This wand was for Milly.

She can even juggle – well, sort of!

Mum knows lots of great games...

At my party we played pin the tail on
the donkey...

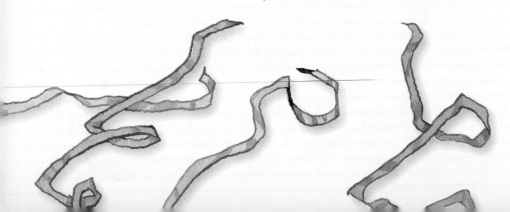

...and musical chairs. I had
to let Jack win!

It's never boring when she is around.

And whenever there is an emergency...

I loved the new ball Milly gave me...

...and so did Bonnie!

...my mum knows exactly what to do.

When I'm feeling sad, my mum can
ALWAYS cheer me up.

I felt sad when it was time for my friends to go home.

Mum tried to be a scary dragon...but she just made me giggle!

She makes everything fun – even tidying up!

Sometimes me and my mum have so much fun,
she gets tired out, and needs a little rest.

James gave me a super set of felt pens.

Mum said I was the loudest dragon
she has ever heard!

Guess who gave me a great pirate storybook?

But she always makes room for me.

Of course, mums come in all sorts of shapes and sizes...

Milly and her mum.

Lucy and her mum.

Jack and his mum.

...but, somehow, MY mum is JUST RIGHT.

Of course, everyone thinks their mum is the best.
But I still think I'm really lucky...

...because I know for sure that MY mum is the
World's Greatest Mum!